The Nodwick

CHRONICLES II
Of Gods and Henchmen

A HENCHMAN COLLECTION OF NODWICK 7-12

BY Aaron Williams

Published by Dork Storm Press

P.O. Box 45063
Madison, WI 53744
E-mail: aaron@nodwick.com

Marketing & Advertising:
Liz Fulda, sales@dorkstorm.com
Phone: 608-255-1348 • Fax: 608-255-1352

Printed in Canada
First Printing, June 2002
ISBN 1-930964-81-1

To my parents
(all four of 'em):

Thank you for being inexplicably
supportive of my aspiration
to not have a *real* job...

TABLE OF CONTENTS

"What is the heaviest thing, ye heroes?
asketh the load-bearing spirit, that I may
take it upon me and rejoice in my strength."

- Friedrich Neitzsche, Thus Spake Zarathustra

DORK STORM

Nodwick ™

$2.95 #7

8

9

10

11

17

18

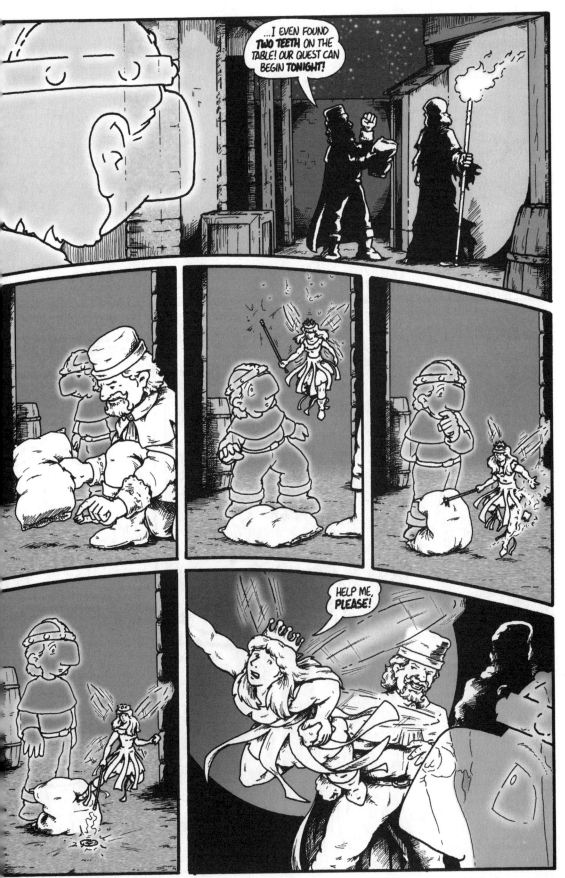

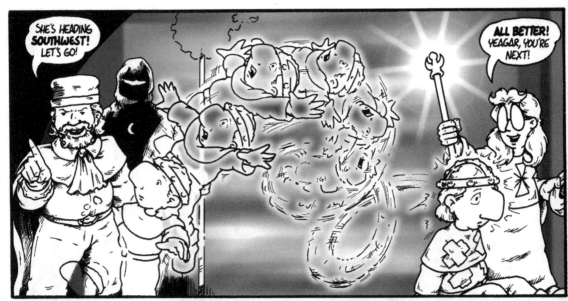

23

24

26

BAPHUMA'AL?! OH, NO...

BARF-O-WHO?

AN OLD FILTHY-YUCK GOD OF EVIL. HE HASN'T BEEN HEARD FROM FOR CENTURIES... BUT IF HE'S BACK...

HE DIDN'T SAY ANYTHING ABOUT BEING AN EVIL GOD... ALTHOUGH THAT MIGHT EXPLAIN HIS AVERSION TO SUNLIGHT... ANYWAY, HE JUST TOLD ME TO HIRE SOMEONE TO GO GET THAT MAGIC PILLOW. THE PILLOW TURNS TEETH INTO GOLD AT THE STROKE OF MIDNIGHT. A FAIRY APPEARS, TAKES THE TEETH, AND LEAVES SOME COINS.

YOU WERE PLANNING TO PUT YOUR PATIENTS' TEETH UNDER THE PILLOW TO MAKE MONEY? IN CASE YOU HAVEN'T HEARD, "GET RICH QUICK" SCHEMES TEND TO PUT THE EMPHASIS ON QUICK.

NAUGHTINESS! HOW MANY INNOCENT PEOPLE WERE YOU GOING TO MAKE TOOTHLESS FOR YOUR WICKED PLAN?

YOU'VE GOT IT ALL WRONG! I WANTED TO FIND OUT WHERE SHE KEEPS ALL OF THE TEETH SHE'S TAKEN AWAY! I'D BE ABLE TO MAKE DENTURES AT NO COST AND SELL THEM FOR A FORTUNE! IF I FOUND WHERE THE COINS CAME FROM AS WELL, SO MUCH THE BETTER.

AND WHAT DID BAPHUMA'AL WANT TO GET OUT OF THE DEAL?

HE DIDN'T SAY, AND I DIDN'T ASK. AT FIRST, I THOUGHT HE WANTED THE GOLD, BUT I GET THE IMPRESSION THAT HE ISN'T MOTIVATED BY MONEY...

POOR NODWICK! WHAT IS THAT DARK NO-GOOD DOING WITH HIM IN THERE?

WAITING FOR MIDNIGHT, I'LL BET...

28

I'M **SO** SORRY ABOUT THIS...

WHAT'S GOING ON? HOW CAN I HELP YOU?

UNTIL MY GOLD SUPPLY RUNS OUT, I'M TIED TO THE PILLOW, A PRISONER OF **DENTAL FISCAL EXCHANGE.** IT'S SUCH A **DRAG.**

HOW DID THIS HAPPEN?

I KIND OF GOT MY DAD **PEEVED** AT ME ABOUT EIGHT HUNDRED YEARS AGO. YOU KNOW THE DESERT CALLED THE **"DUNE FURNACE?"** IT USED TO BE A PART OF A FAIRY KINGDOM BEFORE I... ER, WELL...

YOU DID THAT?!

MY FOLKS WERE OUT OF TOWN, I THREW A PARTY, AND THINGS GOT OUT OF HAND. AS PUNISHMENT, MY DAD GOT A WIZARD TO MAKE ME INTO A **"REAL LIVE TOOTH FAIRY"** AS A GIFT FOR HIS KIDS. HIS CASTLE WAS PLUNDERED BEFORE HE COULD RELEASE ME, AND I'VE BEEN STUCK WITH THE PILLOW EVER SINCE.

LOOK, I'M BEING FORCED TO LEAVE. PLEASE COME HELP ME FIND A WAY **OUT** OF THIS GIG! I'M HELD IN THE RUINS OF A **FAIRY STRONGHOLD** THIRTY LEAGUES TO THE SOUTH!

ENOUGH THALK! I WILL FOLLOW YOU, AND THITH **MORTHAL FOOL** WILL THTAY **HERE,** IF HE VALUETH HITH **THOUL!**

WOW! HE SAID HE WAS GETTING **STRONGER** BUT I THOUGHT HE WAS JUST **BLOWING SMOKE!**

NODWICK! ARE YOU OKAY?

I'M SHORT A **TOOTH,** BUT THE ONE WE SHOULD WORRY ABOUT IS THE **FAIRY!** BAPHUMA'AL IS GOING TO GET WHAT-EVER IT IS HE'S AFTER FROM HER UNLESS WE FIND A WAY TO TRAVEL **THIRTY LEAGUES** IN A HURRY!

YOU AREN'T GOING TO BELIEVE THIS, BUT I'M DETECTING THE AURA OF A **MAGIC CARPET!** IT'S JUST COMING OVER THE HORIZON!

ME, TOO! ARTAX, IF WE CAN **COMBINE** OUR POWERS, WE MIGHT BE ABLE TO DIVERT IT DOWN HERE.

DO IT! WE **STILL** DON'T HAVE OUR ONE THOUSAND GOLD, AND **SOMEONE** IS PONYING UP THE CASH!

HERE IT COMES... GET READY!

YOU'RE **WALKING** HOME. COUNT YOUR-SELF **LUCKY!**

GOODY GUMDROPS FOR US!

WHO WOULD LEAVE A **FLYING CARPET** RUNNING IN THE MIDDLE OF THE NIGHT?

I WOULDN'T LOOK A GIFT CARPET IN THE MOUTH. STILL, IT IS **STRANGE...**

AHEM...

ZAGWICK! I HAVEN'T SEEN YOU SINCE THE **HENCH GAMES!** HAVE YOU BEEN FLYING AROUND UP HERE ALL THIS TIME?

PRETTY MUCH. I'VE TOUCHED GROUND FOR SHORT PERIODS. MOUNTAIN PEAKS, MOSTLY. THEY'RE PRETTY PAINFUL.

I HATE TO BREAK UP THIS REUNION, BUT BAPH-BOY IS **LANDING.**

THEN SO ARE WE!

ISSUE #3

HE MUST BE INSIDE!

LET'S TRY TO GET SOMETHING OUT OF THIS **PILLOW MISSION!**

SORRY ABOUT THE TOUCH-DOWN.

NO PROBLEM. I'M JUST GLAD I CAN KISS THE GROUND WITHOUT **SCRAPING** MY LIPS OFF.

31

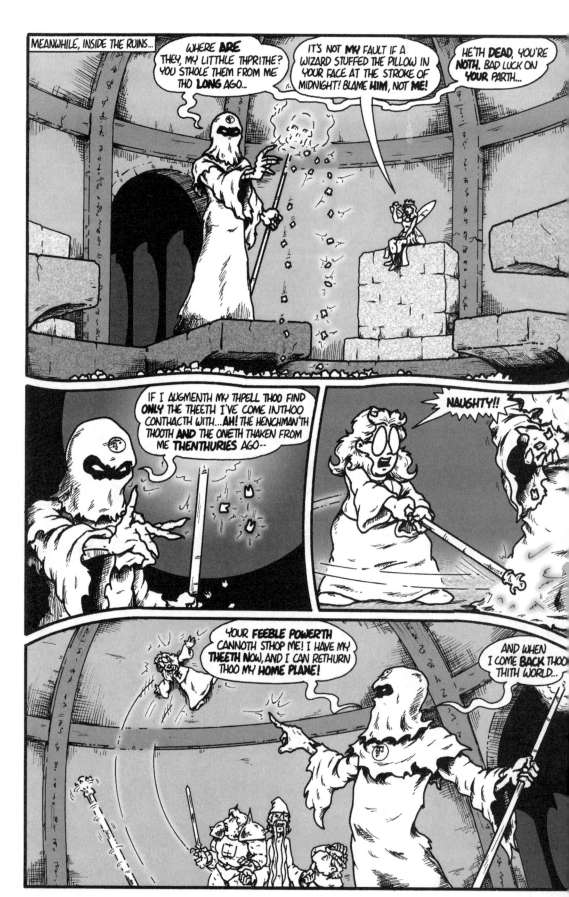

32

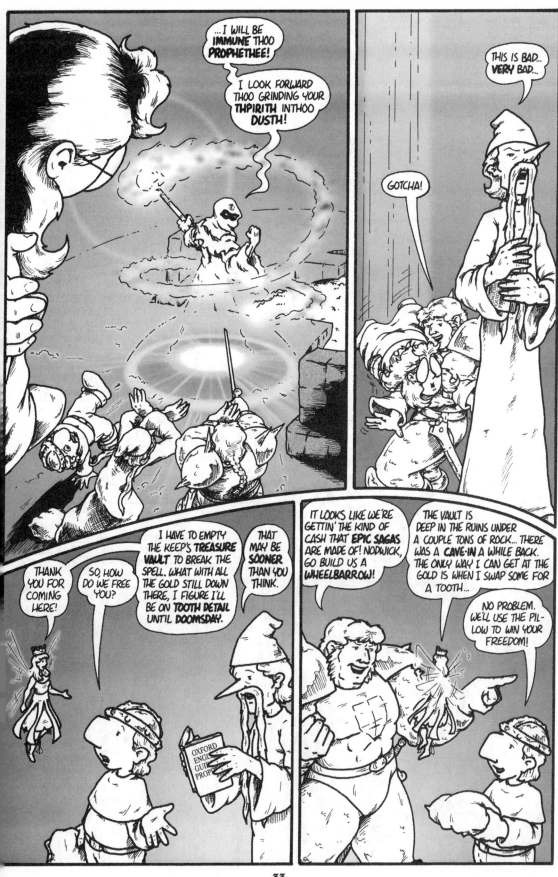

33

DORK STORM

Nodwick

™

2.95 #8

Nodwick in:
The Last Son of Xenon

THE COSMOS. *EVER-CHANGING. INFINITE.*

FORCES HERE SHAPE THE EDGES OF **REALITY** WITH POWERS BEYOND MORTAL COMPREHENSION.

THEY CREATE THE VASTNESS OF **SPACE, TIME,** AND EVEN THOSE BEINGS WHO CALL THEMSELVES **GODS...**

THEY KNOW NO LIMITS...

THEY HAVE NO MASTER...

AND NONE CAN KNOW THEIR PURPOSE...

THEY ARE BEYOND QUESTION, FOR THEY ARE...

THE POWERS WHAT IS!

STKKCH!!

TAP! TAP! TAP!

40

41

42

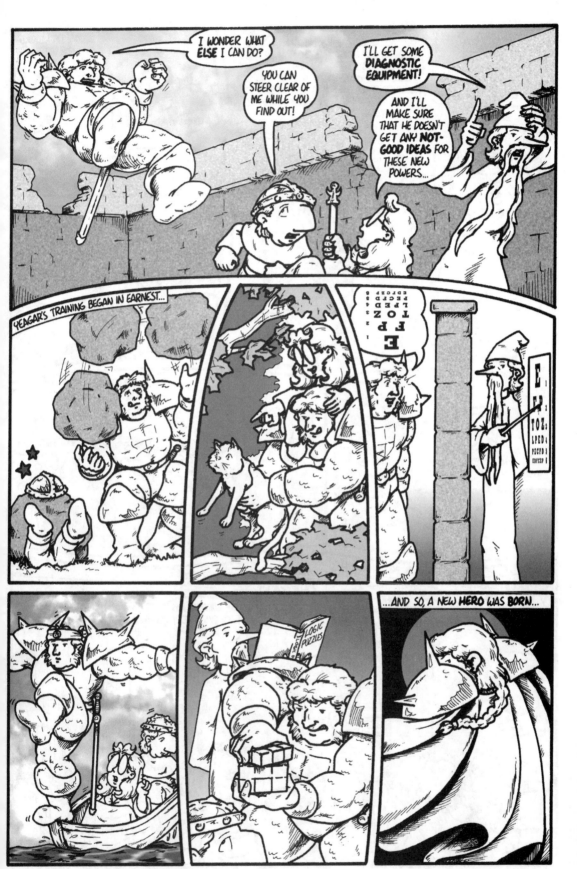

44

45

47

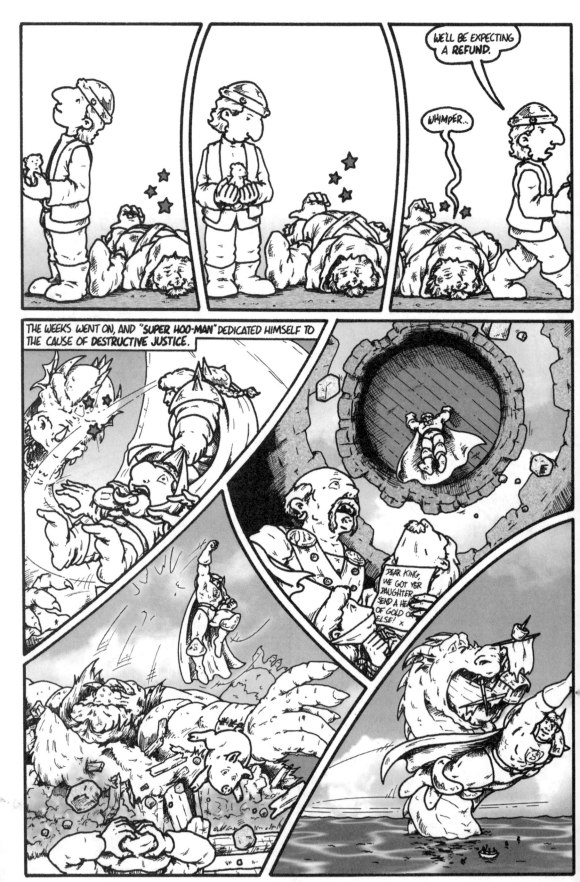

49

51

52

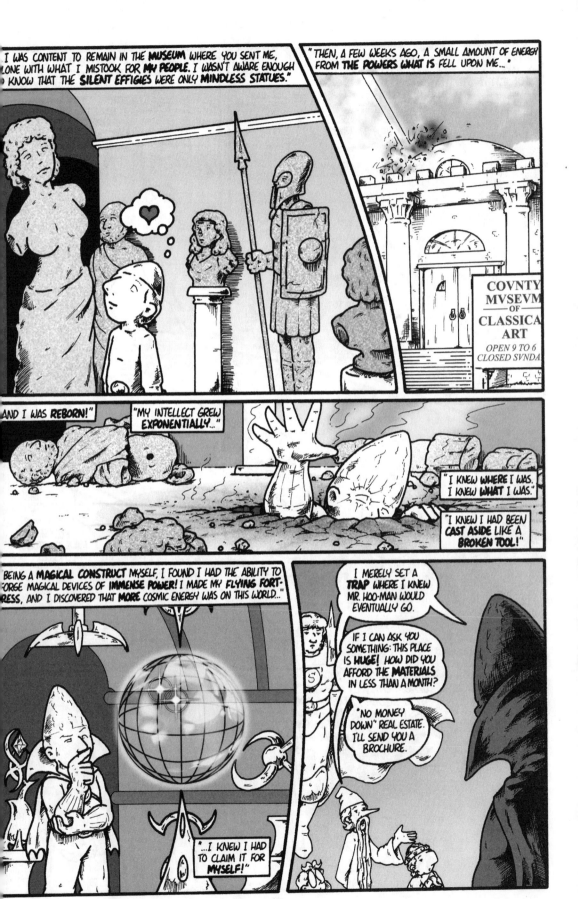

53

55

56

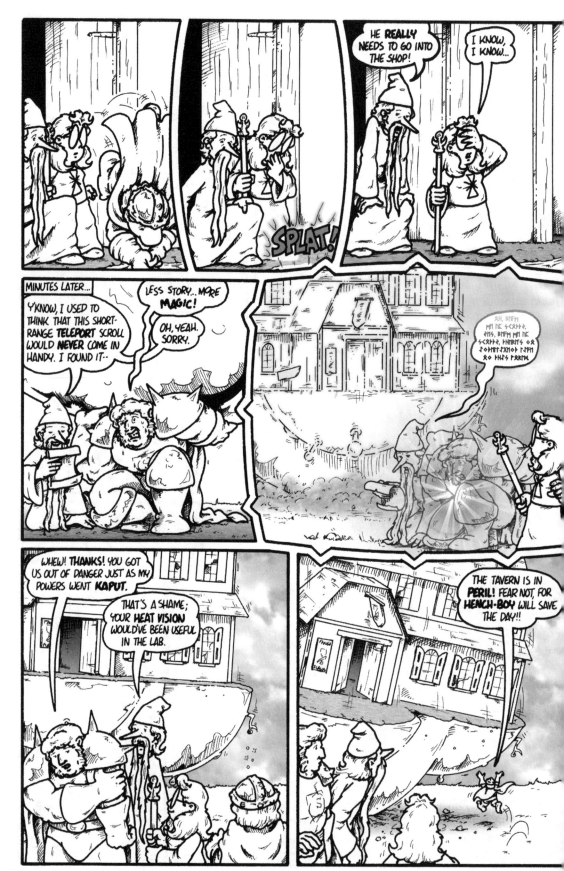

63

65

68

...ODWICK IS UNCEREMONIOUSLY BORNE SKYWARD...

...TOWARDS A CITY THAT SEEMS TO **CONSUME** THE LAND LIKE A **CANCER.**

LEGIONNAIRES! ESCORT THAT **INSECT** TO THE **HALL OF JUDGEMENT!** I'LL INFORM THE **HAND OF BAPHUMA'AL** THAT A PRISONER AWAITS HIS **ATTENTION.**

YOU HAVE THE RIGHT TO CONFESS YOUR TRANSGRESSIONS. ANY DEVIATION FROM THE TRUTH WILL RESULT IN **SWIFT RETRIBUTION** AND POSSIBLY **DEATH.** TELLING THE TRUTH IS NO GUARANTEE OF SAFETY. YOU HAVE THE RIGHT TO **SCREAM** AND **BEG FOR MERCY,** BUT THAT IS OFTEN **COUNTER-PRODUCTIVE.** YOU HAVE THE RIGHT TO **DIE,** BUT NOT UNTIL AN AGENT OF THE STATE HAS UTILIZED A **WEAPON** OF SOME KIND ON YOUR PERSON. DO YOU UNDERSTAND THESE RIGHTS AS THEY HAVE BEEN READ TO YOU?

ER, NOT PARTICULARLY. I--

RIGHTS of the ...OSED

THE QUESTION WAS JUST A FORMALITY ANYWAY.

IT WAS NICE KNOWING YOU!

'BYE!

CLINK

GREAT... THE LAST PERSON I WANT TO SEE IS ANYONE RELATED TO BAPHUMA'AL*

HE MUST BE THE REASON THIS WORLD IS SO CHARMING. I WONDER IF ANYONE TRIED TO STOP HIM--

SO! YOU DARE TO ATTEMPT ESCAPE FROM THE BLACK CITADEL!

*SEE ISSUE #7

WELL, NOT REALLY, BUT IF YOU GIVE ME A HEAD START, I'D BE HAPPY TO GIVE IT A WHIR--

SILENCE!! YOU SHALL-- WAIT... AREN'T YOU A... A HENCHMAN?

UM, YEAH. WHAT--

ALL HENCHMEN WERE WIPED OUT YEARS AGO, OR SO WE THOUGHT! WHAT IS YOUR NAME, WORM?

IT'S, AH, NODWICK, ACTUALLY--

LIAR! IMPOSSIBLE! YOU INSULT ME WITH YOUR FALSEHOODS!!

TOMORROW, I SHALL DEAL WITH YOU PERSONALLY! PREPARE FOR YOUR FINAL SUNRISE, HENCHMAN!

MEANWHILE, BACK IN THE UNIVERSE NEXT DOOR...

GOOD MORNING, SISTER PIFFANY. ARE YOU READY FOR ORIENTATION?

SACRED OECUMENICAL CENOBITINOUS ORDER OF GOODNESS

70

71

72

HOW DO YOU KNOW MY **TRUE NAME**?!

BECAUSE I'VE WORKED WITH Y--ER, I MEAN, BECAUSE I NEVER FORGET A FACE?

YOU **CAN'T** BE NODWICK! HE WAS EATEN BY **GIANT FERAL SHREWS** A FEW DAYS AFTER ARTAX AND I HIRED HIM!

YEAH, BUT PIFFANY PUT ME BACK TOGETHER, REMEMBER?

WHO?

OH. UM... A WANDERING CLERIC. SHE CAME ALONG RIGHT AFTER YOU LEFT ME FOR DEAD...HONEST.

WE COULD'VE USED A DECENT CLERIC. WE WENT THROUGH A **LEGION** OF HENCHMEN AFTER YOU. WE WERE **BANNED** FROM THE ADVENTURER'S GUILD AFTER OUR **EIGHTY-SECOND** ONE.

IF I MAY ASK, WHAT **HAPPENED** TO YOU? I MEAN, YOU **RUN** THIS CITADEL-THING, RIGHT?

WHERE HAVE **YOU** BEEN? I WAS GIVEN THE **POWER TO CONQUER** WHEN I STUCK MY HAND IN THE **GAUNTLET OF SUPREMACY**.

OF COURSE, I HAD TO PLEDGE MYSELF TO **BAPHUMA'AL** IF I WANTED TO AVOID ITS **CURSE**, BUT--

GAPE IN AWE! YOU ARE IN THE PRESENCE OF **ARTAX THE ALL-SEEING AND ALL-KNOWING**!

HEY, ART. GUESS WHO SHOWED UP OUTTA NOWHERE?

NODWICK THE HENCHMAN. DUH. DID YOU MISS MY "ALL-SEEING AND ALL-KNOWING" BIT?

73

WELL, I **AM** JUST A **GLORIFIED GRUNT**, YOU KNOW. YOU HAVE TO USE **SMALL WORDS** IF YOU WANT ME TO UNDERSTAND YOU.

DON'T BE A **SOREHEAD**. JUST PREPARE NODWICK AND HIS BELONGINGS FOR TRANSPORT TO THE **NORTH TOWER**.

THAT WON'T TAKE LONG; HE DIDN'T HAVE ANYTHING ON HIM WHEN WE FOUND HIM.

ODD...

...A **CLOUD** SURROUNDS HIM THAT SEEMS TO OBSCURE... **SOMETHING**...

NOTICE
This box has bee[n] clerically treated s[o] that no force of evil or servants thereof may see it nor open it. See your local clergy for other fine monastic products.

SO! READY TO SEE ARTAX AGAIN, NODWICK?

WHAT? ER, SURE... I GUESS... I THOUGHT... THE SPHERE-- UM, HOW'S HE DOING?

OKAY, I SUPPOSE. IT'S NOT **EASY** SERVING BAPHUMA'AL, BUT IT'S BETTER THAN THE **ALTERNATIVE**...MOST DAYS.

HE'S SERVING BAPHUMA'AL, TOO?

ONE WAY OR ANOTHER, ALMOST **EVERYONE** DOES.

HE'S ALL YOURS, ART!

75

77

CLASS! DON'T MAKE ME USE THE EVIL EXTINGUISHER AGAIN!

CLASS!

CLASS!!

YOU'RE LOOKING... UM... GOOD?

MY APPEARANCE IS IRRELEVANT. I WANT TO KNOW WHY YOU ARE HERE.

WELL, ONE OF YEAGAR'S FLYING SOLDIERS PICKED ME UP AND--

NO. I WANT TO KNOW WHY YOU CAME THROUGH THE CLEFT OF THE COSMOS!

AT FIRST, I BELIEVED YOUR ARRIVAL TO BE A RANDOM OCCURRENCE, BUT MY NEAR-OMNICIENT INTELLECT TELLS ME THERE IS A HIGHER POWER AT WORK.

AND WHO IS ... THIS "PIFFANY" YOU MENTIONED?

SHE'S A CLERIC... AND A TRULY GOOD PERSON. SHE ADVENTURED WITH US IN MY WORLD.

PIFFANY WOULD PATCH US UP WHEN WE GOT HURT... SOME OF US MORE THAN OTHERS...

ODD... NO CLERIC WANTED ANYTHING TO DO WITH YEAGAR AND ME IN OUR ADVENTURING DAYS. YOUR "PIFFANY" MUST HAVE BEEN A UNIQUE INDIVIDUAL.

BUT ENOUGH OF THIS... WE HAVE A BARGAIN TO STRIKE.

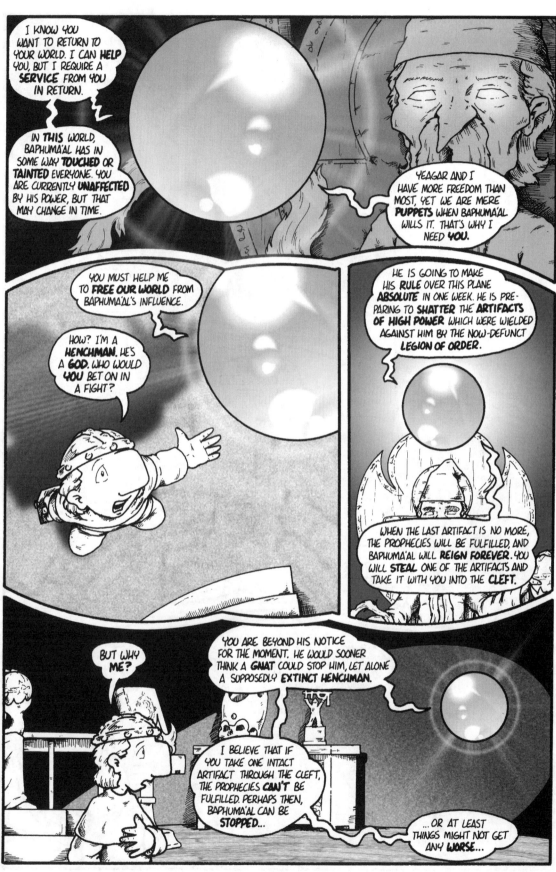

I KNOW YOU WANT TO RETURN TO YOUR WORLD. I CAN **HELP** YOU, BUT I REQUIRE A **SERVICE** FROM YOU IN RETURN.

IN **THIS** WORLD, BAPHUMA'AL HAS IN SOME WAY **TOUCHED** OR **TAINTED** EVERYONE. YOU ARE CURRENTLY **UNAFFECTED** BY HIS POWER, BUT THAT MAY CHANGE IN TIME.

YEAGAR AND I HAVE MORE FREEDOM THAN MOST, YET WE ARE MERE **PUPPETS** WHEN BAPHUMA'AL WILLS IT. THAT'S WHY I NEED **YOU.**

YOU MUST HELP ME TO **FREE OUR WORLD** FROM BAPHUMA'AL'S INFLUENCE.

HOW? I'M A **HENCHMAN.** HE'S A **GOD.** WHO WOULD **YOU** BET ON IN A FIGHT?

HE IS GOING TO MAKE HIS **RULE** OVER THIS PLANE **ABSOLUTE** IN ONE WEEK. HE IS PREPARING TO **SHATTER** THE **ARTIFACTS OF HIGH POWER** WHICH WERE WIELDED AGAINST HIM BY THE NOW-DEFUNCT **LEGION OF ORDER.**

WHEN THE LAST ARTIFACT IS NO MORE, THE PROPHECIES WILL BE FULFILLED, AND BAPHUMA'AL WILL **REIGN FOREVER.** YOU WILL **STEAL** ONE OF THE ARTIFACTS AND TAKE IT WITH YOU INTO THE **CLEFT.**

BUT WHY ME?

YOU ARE BEYOND HIS NOTICE FOR THE MOMENT. HE WOULD SOONER THINK A **GNAT** COULD STOP HIM, LET ALONE A SUPPOSEDLY **EXTINCT HENCHMAN.**

I BELIEVE THAT IF YOU TAKE ONE INTACT ARTIFACT THROUGH THE CLEFT, THE PROPHECIES **CAN'T** BE FULFILLED. PERHAPS THEN, BAPHUMA'AL CAN BE **STOPPED...**

...OR AT LEAST THINGS MIGHT NOT GET ANY **WORSE...**

THAT'S ALL WELL AND GOOD, BUT NEED I REMIND YOU THAT YOU'RE EXPECTED TO HAVE THEM RESPECTING THE LAWS OF THE **LAND** AND THOSE OF THE **GODS** BY THE END OF THE SEMESTER? IF YOU **FAIL**, YOUR STATUS IN THE CHURCH MAY BE...**DOWNGRADED**. YOU MIGHT EVEN LOSE YOUR **DUCT TAPE** PRIVILEGES.

BUT THEY'VE COME SO **FAR** IN ONLY A **WEEK**! I'VE SEEN THE RECORDS OF THE OTHER TEACHERS! EVEN THE ONES WHO **SURVIVED** DIDN'T ACCOMPLISH **THIS** MUCH WITH THOSE **ICKY-BAD NAUGHTY SPAWN** KIDS!

SISTER PIFFANY, WE HAVE **STANDARDS**, AND THEY MUST BE **MET**. WHAT WOULD WE BE IF WE LET THEM **SLIDE**?

WELL, **YES**, BUT FROM WHAT I'VE SEEN, IT'S MOSTLY THEIR **PARENTS** THAT MAKE THEM **NAUGHTY**. HALF OF THE MOMMIES AND DADDIES AREN'T EVEN FROM THIS **DIMENSION**, AND THEY HAVEN'T BEEN ENCOURAGING THEIR KIDS TO DO **NICE THINGS** OR **LEARN TO READ** OR ANYTHING! IF THEY DON'T HAVE **WHOLESOME HOMES**, A LOT OF THINGS I TEACH DON'T SEEM TO **STICK**!

NOW, NOW. WE CAN'T **POSSIBLY** BLAME THE **PARENTS**. I'M SURE THEY DO THEIR **BEST**. NO, THE SUCCESS OR FAILURE OF THE STUDENTS SHOULD **OBVIOUSLY** BE THEIR **TEACHER'S** RESPONSIBILITY.

I GUESS... UM, CAN I ASK ABOUT MY REQUEST FOR **SCHOOL SUPPLIES**? I'VE HAD TO SELL SOME OF MY **POKÉBEANIES** TO BUY PAPER AND PENCILS FOR MY CLASSROOM... I REALLY MISS MY "JUBILIEPUFF" BEANIE...

I ALREADY TOLD YOU: WHEN YOUR KIDS DEMONSTRATE ENOUGH **ACADEMIC IMPROVEMENT**, THEN THE EDUCATION COMMITTEE WILL GIVE YOU THE SUPPLIES YOU ASKED FOR.

OH...

CRACK

IS THAT EVERYTHING, SISTER PIFFANY?

YES. THANK YOU FOR YOUR TIME.

MY DOOR IS **ALWAYS** OPEN.

SAC·RI·FICE! SAC·RI·FICE! BLOOD! BLOOD! BLOOD!

MEANWHILE...

DANG! THAT'S THE **FIFTH** HENCHMAN THIS WEEK!

TELL ME ABOUT IT. UM, WHY DIDN'T YOU WAIT FOR HIM TO GET CLEAR **BEFORE** YOU COLLAPSED THE DUNGEON ENTRANCE?

HEY, DID **YOU** WANT THAT **HORDE OF TROLLS** TO COME OUT AND **GET** US? BESIDES, I DIDN'T HEAR YOU COMPLAINING WHEN WE HAD **NODWICK** TO TOSS AROUND!

THAT'S BECAUSE WE HAD A **CLERIC** WHO COULD REPAIR HIM WHENEVER WE **KILLED** HIM, YOU **DOLT!!**

WHAT? YOU'VE **POWDERED** NODWICK WITH YOUR **STUPID SPELLS** MORE TIMES THAN I CAN **COUNT!**

OH, **REALLY?!** IS THAT A **SINGLE-DIGIT NUMBER** OR HAVE YOU STARTED DOING MATH WITH **ALL** OF YOUR FINGERS?!!

WAIT A MINUTE. THIS IS GETTING US **NOWHERE!** LET'S FACE IT: WE NEED TO GET **PIFFANY** BACK!

AGREED. WE'RE JUST NO GOOD WITHOUT OUR **DUCT-TAPING** COLLEAGUE.

THEN IT'S SETTLED! SO BEGINS OUR **QUEST FOR PIFFANY!!**

To Be Continued...

83

Nodwick in: *A World Without Tiffany* Part II

"TRANSCRIPTION OF TRUTH-STONE SESSION, HOUR TWO: THE HENCHMAN, NODWICK, HAD TRAVELED TO A WORLD **PARALLEL** TO OUR OWN, WHERE THE EVIL GOD, **BAPHUMA'AL**, RULED WITH AN **IRON FIST.**

"TWO OF NODWICK'S FORMER EMPLOYERS, **ARTAX** AND **YEAGAR**, WERE, IN THIS WORLD, **POWERFUL AND FEARSOME PAWNS** OF THE VILE GOD. NODWICK FOUND HIMSELF **ENSNARED** IN A SCHEME TO DISRUPT BAPHUMA'AL'S PLANS WITH THE AID OF A **NEAR-OMNISCIENT** ARTAX. HE HAD SPENT THE BETTER PART OF A **WEEK** GOING OVER THE LAYOUT OF THE **DARK CITADEL** WHERE BAPHUMA'AL WAS TO BEGIN THE **DESTRUCTION** OF **POWERFUL ARTIFACTS** THAT MIGHT **HALT** HIS REIGN...

"STILL IN NODWICK'S POSSESSION WAS A **BOX** OUR ORDER COMMANDED TO BE DROPPED INTO THE **CLEFT OF THE COSMOS** (WHICH IS THE MEANS BY WHICH THE HENCHMAN IN QUESTION WAS TRANS-PORTED TO THE WORLD ADJACENT TO OURS). PROTECTED FROM **EVIL**, THE BOX REMAINED **UNDETECTED** BY PRACTICALLY **EVERYONE** NODWICK ENCOUNTERED...

"WE NOW CONTINUE THE INTERROGATION CONCERNING EVENTS LEADING UP TO THE ATTEMPTED **THEFT** OF ONE OF THE APPARENTLY **DOOMED** MAGICAL ARTIFACTS..."

88

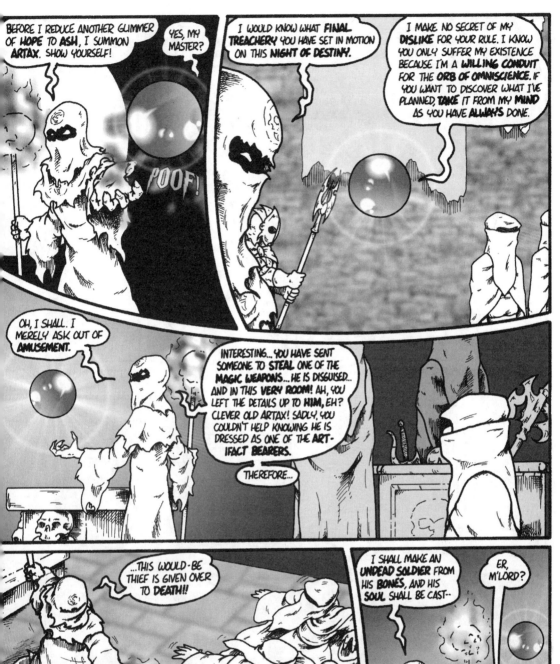

BEFORE I REDUCE ANOTHER GLIMMER OF **HOPE** TO **ASH**, I SUMMON **ARTAX**. SHOW YOURSELF!

YES, MY MASTER?

POOF!

I WOULD KNOW WHAT **FINAL TREACHERY** YOU HAVE SET IN MOTION ON THIS **NIGHT OF DESTINY.**

I MAKE NO SECRET OF MY **DISLIKE** FOR YOUR RULE. I KNOW YOU ONLY SUFFER MY EXISTENCE BECAUSE I'M A **WILLING CONDUIT** FOR THE **ORB OF OMNISCIENCE.** IF YOU WANT TO DISCOVER WHAT I'VE PLANNED, **TAKE** IT FROM MY **MIND** AS YOU HAVE **ALWAYS** DONE.

OH, I SHALL. I MERELY ASK OUT OF AMUSEMENT.

INTERESTING... YOU HAVE SENT SOMEONE TO **STEAL** ONE OF THE **MAGIC WEAPONS**...HE IS DISGUISED... AND IN THIS **VERY ROOM!** AH, YOU LEFT THE DETAILS UP TO **HIM**, EH? CLEVER OLD ARTAX! SADLY, YOU COULDN'T HELP KNOWING HE IS DRESSED AS ONE OF THE **ART-IFACT BEARERS.**

THEREFORE...

...THIS WOULD-BE THIEF IS GIVEN OVER TO **DEATH!!**

I SHALL MAKE AN **UNDEAD SOLDIER** FROM HIS **BONES**, AND HIS **SOUL** SHALL BE CAST--

ER, M'LORD?

WORKS FOR ME!

POOF!

FULL MARBLE COMPANY

Come to us when you've lost your marbles.

ARTAX?

MASTER?

CONGRATULATIONS. YOU'VE FINALLY MADE ME ANGRY ENOUGH TO PUNISH YOU. AS SOON AS MY BODY RE-FORMS, YOU'RE GOING TO REGRET HAVING A NERVOUS SYSTEM.

THANK YOU, MASTER.

COMPANY

...PAST THE VAULT OF SKULLS, OVER THE PITS OF TORMENT, THROUGH THE DESANGUINATION BATHS...

...'ROUND THE FOYER OF FLAYED FLESH, AND OUT THE MAIN GATE!!

...WHICH IS HEAVILY GUARDED...

PIK!

I MIGHT HAVE TO STOP USING THIS THING; I'M STARTING TO LIKE IT...

94

95

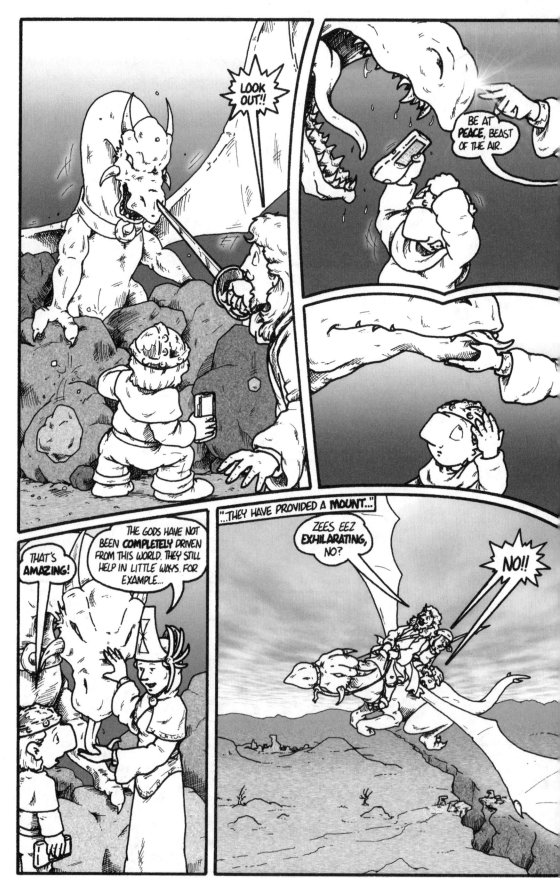

TH THE THUNDER OF BAPHUMA'AL'S **RAGE** SHAKING THE VERY ONES AROUND HIM, NODWICK **LEAPT** INTO THE **CLEFT**...

...AND DISCOVERED THE **WAY HOME** ISN'T ALWAYS A **DIRECT ROUTE**...

GLURK.

YEP, THAT TEARS IT. I'M SWITCHING TO DECAF.

HI. COULD YOU BE A PAL AND JIGGLE THE HANDLE IN HERE FOR ME? I'M TRYING TO GET BACK TO MY HOME UNIVERSE.

MEN

Y'KNOW, I'M **REALLY** GETTING TIRED OF ALL THE **GRATUITOUS CROSSOVERS** THEY'RE PUTTING IN COMIC BOOKS THESE DAYS...

THEN AGAIN, I COULD BE COMPLETELY WRONG.

PIFFANY! IT'S GREAT TO SEE YOU AGAI--

OH, IT'S AWFUL HERE! THEY GAVE ME A CLASSROOM FULL OF THE MOST EVIL CHILDREN TO BE INSTRUCTED IN THE WAYS OF GOODNESS AND VIRTUE, BUT THEY JUST CAN'T BE REFORMED! THEY BITE, THEY SCRATCH, THEY MAKE VILE INCANTATIONS, THEY SUMMON BEASTS FROM THE DARKEST PLANES AND THEY'RE S ICKY-BAD NASTY THAT I JUST WANNA SCREAM NOT-NICE WORDS AND STUFF!! WHAT'S WORSE, IF THEY DON'T IMPROVE SOON, I'LL PROBABLY WASH OUT OF MY CLERICAL ORDER

THIS SOUNDS LIKE SOMETHING WE CAN HANDLE.

WHERE DO YOU KEEP THE LITTLE TYKES?

SOON...

HEY! THEY LOOK LIKE THE CROWD I RAN WITH WHEN I WAS A KID!

JUST HANG LOOSE, PIFFANY. WE'LL TAKE CARE OF THIS, NO PROBLEM.

106

GOOD MORNIN', KIDDOS! WHO CAN TELL ME THE DIFFERENCE BETWEEN A **FELONY** AND A **MISDEMEANOR**?

MISS PIFFANY? YOU HAVE ANOTHER VISITOR.

MINUTES LATER...

REVEREND MATRON?

AH, MISS PIFFANY! DID YOU TAKE CARE OF THOSE **HOODLUMS** WHO ATTACKED MY TEA-ROOM?

SORT OF. ANYWAY, WE HAVE ANOTHER PROBLEM WE NEED TO DEAL WITH.

UM, HELLO, YOUR...UM, REVERENDNESS. NOT TO BE **DISRESPECTFUL** OR ANYTHING, BUT YOU HAVE TO LET PIFFANY GO ADVENTURING WITH HER FRIENDS. THE FATE OF THE **WORLD** DEPENDS ON IT!

MY, SUCH A **DRAMATIC STATEMENT!** I TAKE IT YOU HAVE **PROOF** OF THIS, DO YOU NOT? I CANNOT TAKE THE WORD OF A MERE **HENCHMAN** AND LET ONE OF MY MOST **VALUABLE** CLERICS WASTE EVEN **MORE** OF HER TIME AND SKILLS ON **SILLY QUESTS.**

LOOK, I TRAVELLED THROUGH MORE WORLDS THAN I CAN **COUNT** TO GET BACK HERE! I'VE **SEEN** WHAT MIGHT HAPPEN IF PIFFANY DOESN'T KEEP AN EYE ON **ARTAX** AND **YEAGAR!**

I'M SORRY, BUT WITHOUT **EVIDENCE**...

WELL, THERE **IS** A WAY TO BE CERTAIN...

WHATEVER IT IS, I'LL **DO IT!!**

The End

110

DORK STORM

$2.95 #11

Nodwick ™

114

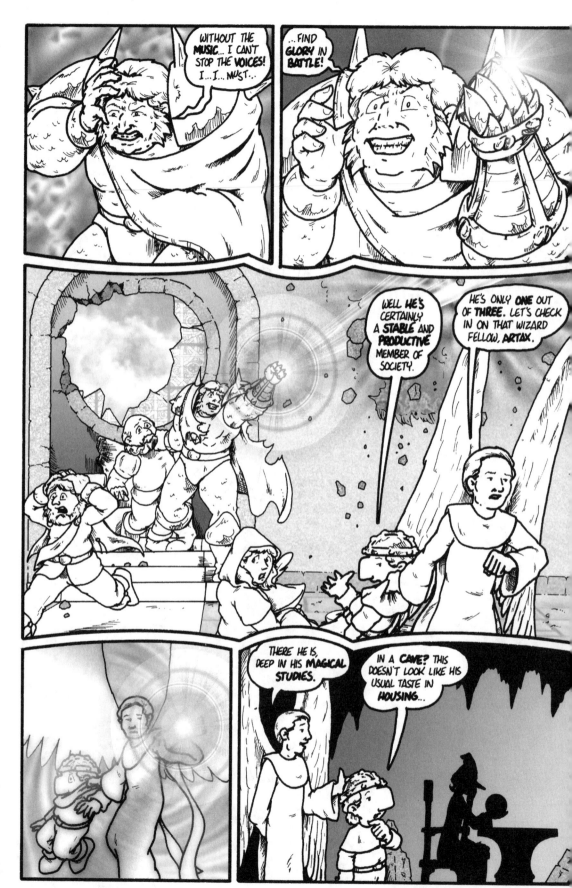

WELL, I JUST WANTED TO EXPLAIN THAT THIS WHOLE FIASCO ISN'T CLARENCE'S FAULT, ENTIRELY. THERE'S NOTHING HE COULD DO, EVEN IF I WANTED TO GO INTO THE GREAT BEYOND. I'M BOUND BY MY HENCHMAN EMPLOYMENT CONTRACT TO "REMAIN ON THIS PLANE OF EXISTENCE EVEN IF PULMONARY AND CARDIOVASCULAR FUNCTIONS CEASE, SO LONG AS HOPE OF REVIVIFICATION EXISTS OR ONE YEAR AFTER DATE OF DEATH, WHICHEVER IS LONGER.

SO IT'S PRETTY MUCH A MOOT POINT.

WE SEE...

VERY WELL. WE'LL OVERLOOK THIS ON HIS RECORD. STILL, SEE IF YOU CAN'T COME UP WITH SOME FAVOR HE CAN DO FOR YOU. IF HE DOESN'T DO SOMETHING POSITIVE, HE'LL MOPE ABOUT IT FOR CENTURIES.

I'LL TALK IT OVER WITH HIM. I ADMIRE YOUR WORK, ESPECIALLY THE SUNSETS.

THANKS. IT TOOK FOREVER TO GET THE PURPLES JUST RIGHT. GOODBYE.

SO, WHAT NOW?

WELL, IT'S ALMOST YULETIDE, AND I STILL HAVE ONE GIFT TO FIND...

SOON...

THERE! ALL BETTER!

THE FLAMEBELCH WYRM'S TREASURE HOARD WILL FILL OUR YULETIDE SHOPPING LIST IN SPADES! I THINK I EVEN FOUND A GIFT THAT WILL CONVINCE THE "FANG AND FLAGON" TO RE-OPEN MY TAB!

AND I CAN BUY PLENTY OF MAGIC COMPONENTS FOR THE WIZARD GUILD GIFT EXCHANGE. I'LL WHIP UP SOME SPELL SCROLLS THAT'LL KNOCK THEIR SOCKS OFF!

JUST SO LONG AS ENOUGH GOLD IS LEFT FOR THE **ORPHAN'S YULETIDE JUBILEE.** I'M NOT GOING TO HAVE TO **PRY UP THE FLOOR-BOARDS** TO FIND WHERE YOU'VE HIDDEN OUR TREASURE, AGAIN, AM I?

NO, MA'AM.

GOOD! WELL, LET'S HEAD FOR HOME. I THINK WE STILL HAVE SOME YUMMY **APPLE CIDER** WE CAN HEAT UP TONIGHT!

DO YOU THINK SHE'D LOOK ON THE **ROOF?**

...S LATER, **YULETIDE EVE** HAS COME, AND CELEBRATIONS ARE IN FULL SWING...

I'M OFF TO THE JUBILEE! I THINK ARTAX AND YEAGAR ARE ON THE ROOF, DOING SOME LAST-MINUTE DECORATION.

I'M HEADED TO THE HENCHMAN'S UNION HALL FOR A PARTY, MYSELF. BUT WE CAN'T DEPART JUST YET...

MERRY YULE, PIFFANY. THANKS FOR KEEPING ME GOING ALL THIS TIME.

OH, BUT YOU DIDN'T HAVE TO!

BE SURE TO OPEN IT BEFORE YOU LEAVE. SEE YOU LATER!

126

129

131

OUR HEROES EMERGE FROM THE DEPTHS...

HEY, THERE! DID Y'ALL GET A GOOD LOOK AT WHAT THE **HOLLOW OF HAZARDOUS HORROR** HAS TO OFFER?

ARE Y'ALL INTERESTED IN SIGNIN' THE **MORTGAGE** FOR THIS **FINE FACILITY**?

NAH, WE'LL PASS. WITHOUT WALL-TO-WALL CARPET, I CAN'T SEE US BUYING IT.

YEAH. IT NEE[D] MORE **WINDO[W] TREATMENT** TOO.

THAT'S TOO BAD. I FIGURED YOU'D FIND **SOMETHIN'** IN THERE THAT'D GRAB YOUR INTEREST...

WE'RE STEALING THE **STAR** OF **ELYSIVANA** AND I CAN'T **LIE** EVEN IF IT'S TO AN **OBVIOUSLY** NASTY BAD MAN LIKE **YOU** SO I FEEL THE RIGHT THING TO DO IS TO **BUY** YOUR HOLLOW TO MAKE IT UP TO YOU!!

HONESTLY, SHE HELD OUT A **LOT** LONGER THAN I THOUGHT SHE WOULD.

WE'RE GOING TO HAVE TO RAID ABOUT **THIRTY** DRAGON'S LAIRS TO **PAY** FOR THIS DUMP!!

I'M **SORRY**, GUYS, BUT YOU ASKED ME TO **LET DOWN** THOSE MONSTER-PEOPLE AND HELP **STEAL** SOMETHING IN THE **SAME DAY**!

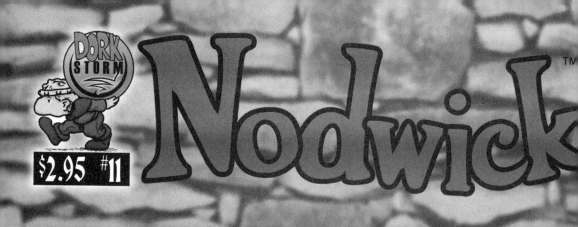

136

137

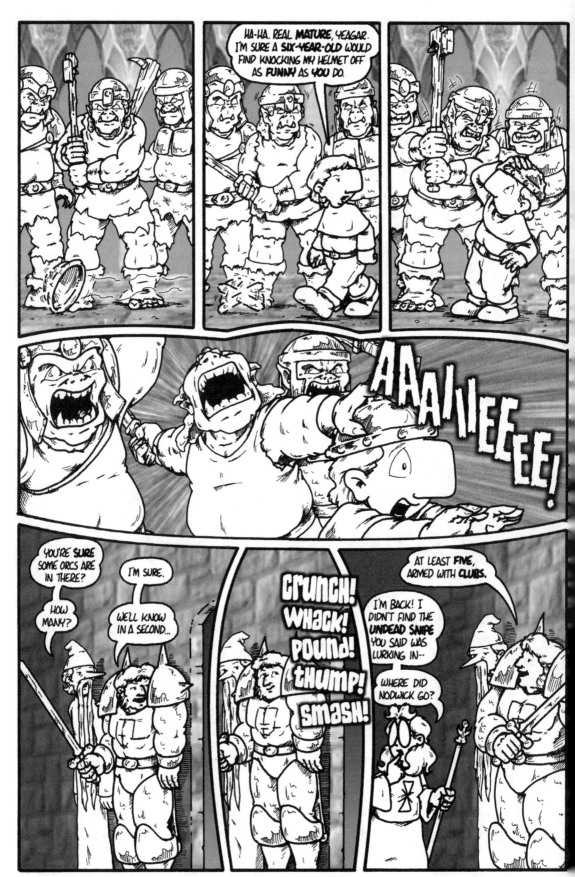

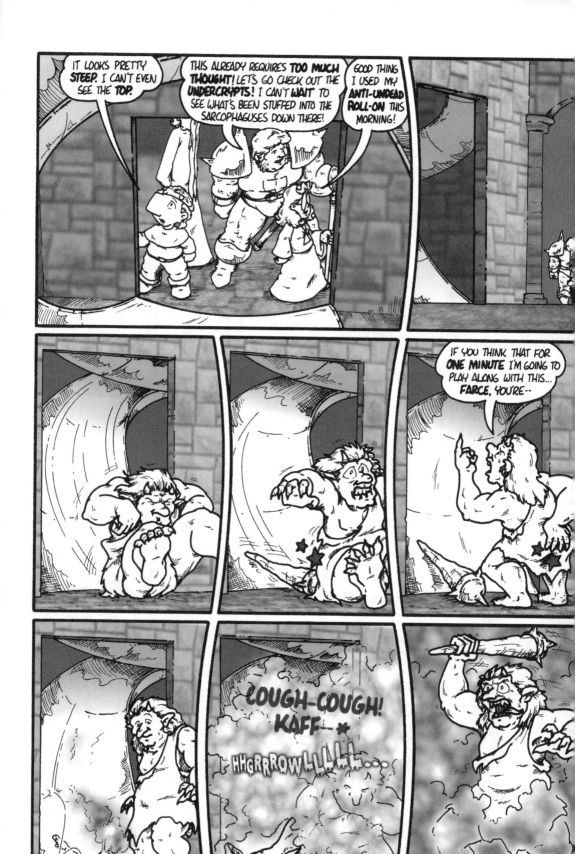

141

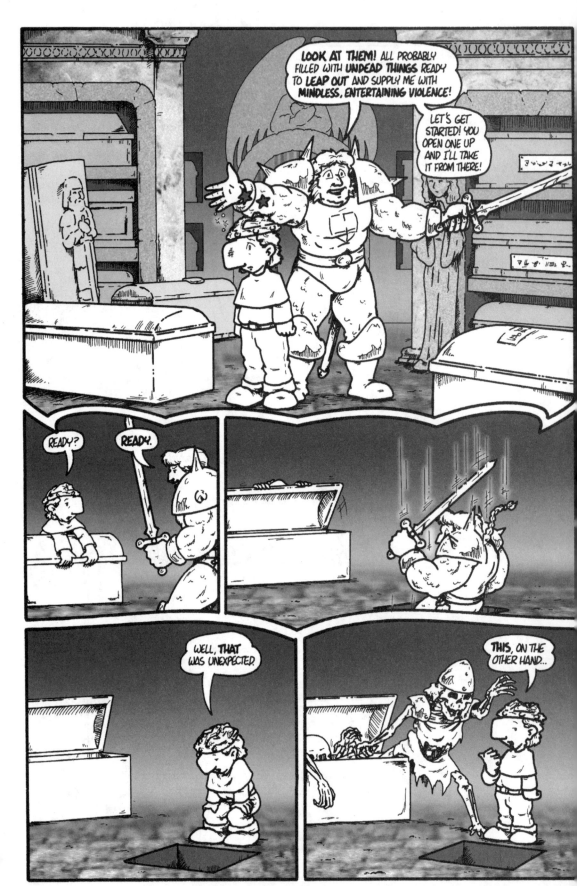

144

145

YEAGAR AND COMPANY SOON FORGOT THE TROLL'S MYSTERIOUS TATTOO...

SMASH 'N' SLASH!

GOODNESS AND HAPPY PUPPIES SHALL PREVAIL!

EAT MYSTIC ENERGIES, REPTILE!

SO DID YOU ENJOY THEIR HEROIC DIALOGUE? WAS IT TOO CLICHÉ? BE HONEST...

THAT'S ANOTHER ROOM CLEARED!

WOW! THIS DUNGEON IS A LOT LESS STRESSFUL THAN THE FIRST TIME WE EXPLORED IT.

WE'VE IMPROVED WITH AGE. SAY, NODWICK, WHAT'S OUR TREASURE HAUL LOOKING LIKE?

WELL, LET'S SEE... SINCE WE LAST TOOK STOCK, WE'VE ACQUIRED THREE ROYAL SIGNET RINGS, FOUR TIARAS, A GOLD SEAL FROM THE COURT OF ANSERINIA, TWO JEWELED CROWNS, A SET OF "KELDORIAN ORDER OF REGAL KNIGHTHOOD" SWORDS, AND A RUBY NECKLACE INSCRIBED "TO MY BELOVED PRINCESS HELEXIA."

AM I THE ONLY ONE SEEING SOMETHING UNUSUAL HERE?

WELL--

SHUT UP! OH, LOOK! A TRAIL OF BLOOD HURRY, SOMETHING'S GETTING AWAY!

146

148

149

I THOUGHT OF TWO ANIMALS. WAS THAT OKAY?
FINE, JUST FINE.
WHAT IS THIS, ANYWAY?
IT'S A COMPOUND SYNTHESIZED FROM MORPHEUS MOLD, COMBINED WITH SEVERAL POWERFUL SPELLS. I'VE NEVER SEEN IT IN THIS QUANTITY BEFORE...
THEY USED IT ON ME!
I USED TO BE THE ARCHDUKE OF CRAGEN MOOR! NOW I'M... THIS.
NO OFFENSE, BUT I HEARD YOU WERE...UM, KIND OF A DESPOT. YOU HAD ONE OF THE HIGHEST TYRRANY RATINGS IN "FEUDAL WEEKLY."
THAT'S NOTHING! COMPARED TO SOME OF THE PEOPLE IN HERE, I'M A SAINT! THAT'S BRAGAN THE RED OVER THERE. OVER TEN SIBLINGS BETWEEN HIM AND HIS FATHER'S THRONE WOUND UP FLOATING IN HIS MOAT!
SOUNDS LIKE SOMEONE'S LOCKING UP ICKY-BAD ROYAL PEOPLE!
NOT NECCESSARILY, PIFFANY. I'VE TALKED TO THE OTHER CAPTIVES, AND A LOT OF THEM SEEM TO BE JUST CLUELESS NOBLES. THEY'D BE ANNOYING TO HAVE AROUND, BUT FOR THE MOST PART, THEY'RE HARMLESS.
HARMLESS UNTIL THEY'RE TURNED INTO MONSTERS, THAT IS.
AND GASSED SO THEY'LL GO BERSERK. IT MAKES A WEIRD KIND OF SENSE--
CLICK
CREEEAA

151

PIFFANY'S **DUCT TAPE** REVIVED THE FALLEN **DUNGEON DENIZENS**...

...WHILE ARTAX USED THE **MORPHEUS DUST** TO RESTORE THEIR BOD...

OKAY, YOU'VE ALL BEEN GIVEN A **SECOND CHANCE** AT LIFE. I ADVISE YOU TO FIND **QUIET LIVES** SOMEWHERE **FAR AWAY** FROM WHERE YOU USED TO LIVE SINCE SOMEONE THERE TRIED TO DO **ICKY-BAD STUFF** TO YOU. IS EVERYONE GOOD WITH THAT? ALL RIGHTY THEN, **BYE-BYE!**

SO YOU SEE, SOMEONE HAS BEEN USING THIS PLACE TO DISPOSE OF **ANNOYING** OR **INCONVENIENT** NOBILITY. THEY WERE **KIDNAPPED, TRANSFORMED** IN... **MONSTERS**, DROPPED INTO THE **LABYRINTH** A... **GASSED** INTO A STATE OF **TOTAL RAGE**. ADVENTURERS LIKE US WOULD **OFF** THEM, AND NO ONE WOULD BE THE WISER.

OH.

BUT WE'RE KEEPING THE LOOT, RIGHT?

OF COURSE. DON'T BE SILLY.

154

155

ACKNOWLEDGMENTS

Special thanks go out to Phil Foglio, John Kovalic, and Scott Kurtz for making the joke on page 103 possible. I hope we get to participate in a few more gratuitous crossovers soon. I also want to thank everyone who sent me words of encouragement to finish Issue #10 and make darn sure that it had a happy ending "or else." Thanks to Liz Fulda for helping me get this volume printed. Thanks to the people who run the Egyptian Campaign in Carbondale, Ill for being so understanding when I realized I left my latest issue at home. Thanks to the RPGKC crowd for letting me attend their cons to hawk my wares. Stuart McDaniel gets a big pile of gratitude for running the online fan-club, and thanks to everyone else who I'm almost certainly forgetting. Hench on!

Special thanks to Darell Johnson who was kind enough to provide the quote on page 5.

ABOUT THE AUTHOR

At the tender age of ten, Aaron Williams was exposed to Dungeons & Dragons, and his Charles Shultz-inspired drawing found a new direction. His first one-panel cartoon was published by Dragon Magazine in 1989. His path to the Dark Side was now paved in ink. He went on to have fairly regular cartoon appearances in the pages of Dragon. Turning to more comedic subjects, Aaron created a large-nosed henchman named Nodwick, gave him some of the most oddball adventurers to be employed by, and the rest is history. Nodwick continues to amuse and get maimed in the pages of Dragon Magazine, Dungeon Magazine, Nodwick Comics, and on Gamespy.com. He is also working on bringing a new feature to comics: ps238.

In spite of what his friends tell him, he still thinks he's funny.

REST INDEX PEACE

The following catalogues a handful of the many incidents where the henchman known as Nodwick either met his end, or soon would have if not for the ministrations of the legendary cleric, Piffany.

Entries followed by a "†" symbol reference pages in Volume I

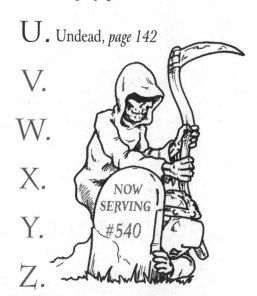

NOW SERVING #540

...and the hench-adventure continues...